Look At Me!

By Joyce Zemke
Illustrated by Maureen Shaughnessy

Journeys
Level One

Jaap Tuinman

PROGRAM EDITOR
Kathleen Doyle

Ginn and Company
Educational Publishers

© Copyright 1984 by Ginn and Company,
a Division of Xerox Canada Inc.

C97027   ISBN 0-7702-1281-6   Printed and bound in Canada   .BCDEFGH   8987654

"I am red,"
said the wagon.

"Look at me!"

"I am yellow,"
said the flower.

"Look at me!"

3

"I am green,"
said the leaf.

"Look at me!"

4

"I am blue,"
said the car.

"Look at me!"

"I am red
and yellow
and green
and blue,"
said the rainbow.

6

"Look at me!"

⑦

I Like This Book

By William Jay Smith
Illustrated by Leoung O'Young

"I like this book," said the King of Spain.
"I think I'll read it through again."

From *Laughing Time* by William Jay Smith. Copyright © 1953, 1955, 1956, 1957, 1959, 1968, 1974, 1977 by William Jay Smith.